W9-CYB-186

JANNOT A FRENCH RABBIT

by

Mireille Marokvia

Illustrated by Artur Marokvia

Pet rabbits in France were usually called Jannot, and this was the name of Ann's black rabbit. She and her friend, Paul, took good care of Jannot, even kept a silver bell around his neck, in case he got lost. One day, through no fault of Ann's, Jannot got away. He found a rabbits' paradise, the baker's garden. He started on thyme and lavender and then moved on to the peaceful garden of the priest, and on to other gardens. Everywhere the silver bell tinkled until all the people, including the mayor, were puzzled about the bell. Ann and Paul looked for him, and worried whether someone would catch Jannot. He had a wonderful time in the little French village and when the children did find him, he was a wiser rabbit, and so were they wiser children!

* *

Dewey Decimal Classification: F

About the Author:

MIREILLE MAROKVIA was born in a small village near Chartres, France. After boarding school she went to a teachers' college, then studied at the Sorbonne in Paris. She began to write while quite young, and when she was nineteen had an article published. She taught for a while in Paris, did editorial work, and much translating of novels and medical articles. A book of her short stories was brought out in Germany. She came to the United States in 1950, and studied at Columbia University. She also worked in the dress design world of Seventh Avenue, but has returned to her first love, writing.

About the Illustrator:

ARTUR MAROKVIA, who is Mireille Marokvia's husband, is a well-known painter and illustrator. Before he turned to art, however, he was a pianist in Germany, an engineer in Italy and a student of ballet in Paris. He was born in Germany, and spent his childhood there and in Italy and France, studying in Germany and in Paris. He has also lived in Greece, Yugoslavia, Finland, Russia, Spain and Austria. He came to the United States in 1949.

JANNOT
A FRENCH RABBIT

written by
MIREILLE MAROKVIA
with drawings by
ARTUR MAROKVIA

1964 FIRST CADMUS EDITION
THIS SPECIAL EDITION IS PUBLISHED BY ARRANGEMENT WITH
THE PUBLISHERS OF THE REGULAR EDITION
J. B. LIPPINCOTT COMPANY
BY
E. M. HALE AND COMPANY
EAU CLAIRE, WISCONSIN

COPYRIGHT © 1959 BY MIREILLE MAROKVIA AND ARTUR MAROKVIA
LIBRARY OF CONGRESS CATALOG CARD NUMBER 58-59934

This edition lithographed in U. S. A. by Wetzel Bros., Inc., Milwaukee 2, Wisconsin

ONCE, in a small French village where the houses
clustered around the church, a rabbit was born. He
was black all over except for his four feet that were
as white as snow. He had many sisters and brothers,
but he was by far the strongest.

When he was barely six weeks old he was taken out
of his mother's pen and put into a basket cushioned
with hay. His owner, an old lady in her black Sunday
dress and her white bonnet, climbed on to the seat of
a donkey cart, and away they drove. They drove on a
gravel road beside a swiftly running brook and beside
pastures where big gray horses and brown cows
were grazing.

During the trip the rabbit lay quietly in a corner of
his basket. This was not easy because the cart was not
going smoothly on the gravel road. Suddenly there
was a big jolt because of a sharp turn, then they slowly
climbed a hill. At last they entered another village,
sunny and silent, where the houses clustered around
the church . . . as usual.

6

The houses were small, but each had a large garden, an orchard, a chicken yard, a rabbit's house, and a good fence around everything.

The donkey stopped, and a dog barked loud greetings. At that a little girl, in her white Sunday apron, ran out of the house. She kissed the donkey on his velvet nose, she kissed her grandmother as she climbed down from the cart, she peeked into the basket . . . and kissed the black rabbit.

"Ann, my little one," said her grandmother, "you are getting big and wise. I wonder if you are wise enough to take care of a rabbit all by yourself."

"Oh yes!" Ann thought she was.

"Watch out for the 'bad grass,'" warned grandmother. "You know what it does to rabbits . . . and to little girls, and mothers, and fathers as well, don't you? It puts them to sleep . . . for good."

Ann wondered how one could tell "bad grass" from "good grass." She asked her little friend Paul, the neighbors' son, who had just come to play, as he always did. He was already in school and said he knew all about grass. He set to work at once. On a piece of cardboard he painted five plants that were good for rabbits; crimson clover, wild white clover, yellow clover, dandelion and plantain. Then, in red, he painted the "bad grass," the poisonous hemlock that grew over fields and gardens.

"You have to remember it is not red, but green, and looks very much like parsley, or chervil, or carrot leaves," said Paul.

All the time Paul was working, Ann held the rabbit in her arms and fed him carrots and white bread.

Then he was taken to his house, which was large enough to shelter a lamb or two, with a wide screened window looking on the chicken yard. He was given a bed made of fresh yellow straw trimmed with daisies and violets. He had bowls for water and milk, and plates for bran and oats, and a trough for grass. And he was given a name Jannot—which is the name usually given to pet rabbits in France. And he had a silver bell tied around his neck. He did not mind the name, but he shook his head disapprovingly when the bell was tied around his neck. Even when he was told that his bell would come in handy, if he should ever get lost, he shook his head.

9

Jannot was well taken care of. Every day Ann picked grass for him. She was always afraid of giving him the "bad grass." Once she dreamed that she had done so. She got out of bed in a hurry and ran through the garden in her nightgown. But Jannot, very much alive indeed, was standing on his hind legs, pushing his nose against the window screen and waiting for the bread that he knew was hidden in Ann's apron pocket.

Jannot grew so fast that his collar had to be adjusted twice before the summer.

Ann was proud of him. And so was Paul.

But something, of course, had to happen.

It was on a very hot Sunday afternoon in July, when everyone wisely was taking a nap: friends and parents in their cool houses, dogs on doorsteps, cats in the raspberry bushes, chickens in the dust under a tree, birds in the foliage . . . everyone, except the big golden sun and Ann. The little girl wanted to play with her black rabbit.

The black rabbit himself was not ready for play. Not at all. He was lying in the darkest corner of his house, his long stiff legs stretched out, his eyes closed. He did not move at all when Ann came. The way he lay frightened Ann, and she thought of the "bad grass." Her throat felt so tight, she could not even say, "Hello, Jannot." And there was a big pain in her heart. For a while she stood as motionless as the rabbit.

Then an old hen, perhaps talking in her dreams, cried, "What, what?" The rooster opened one yellow round eye, stared at the little girl. "Oh, oh!" he said.

That was all she needed to make her run. She ran, ran, ran through yard and garden. At last she crawled under the laurel bush where she had a summerhouse for her dolls. Her dog found her there. He wanted to know what was the matter but all she could do was cry. So he wiped her face again and again with his big pink tongue. They both got very tired and at last they fell asleep.

They woke up only when Paul arrived carrying a bunch of crimson clover and the last tender dandelion of the season.

"Jannot does not need food anymore," said Ann.

"Why? Is he dead?" asked Paul.

"He is sleeping for good," she corrected. "And soon he will be in the rabbits' paradise."

"We have to bury him, then," said the boy.

"No, no, no," cried Ann.

And since she seemed to be ready to burst into tears any minute Paul agreed with her. Yes, Jannot was on his way to the rabbits' paradise. No, there would be no burying. No, they would not play near his place any more. No, they would not talk about him at all . . . ever.

And this is how Jannot was abandoned.

He got no food, and he got no drink.

He did not call for help as a chicken, or a cat, or a dog would. But when he got hungry enough, he began to munch the bottom of his door which, luckily, was old and soft.

In no time at all he had munched his way into the rabbits' paradise—the garden.

The menu there was out of this world. The bed, prepared between thyme and lavender under a canopy of sunflowers, was softer than a cloud. And the peace, thanks to the fence that kept out dogs and other enemies, was heavenly.

All around, farther than one could see, there were other paradises separated from each other by fences and hedges.

A rabbit could squeeze through them or dig a hole under them. At midnight Jannot popped out of a neat tunnel—white feet and black nose a little bit dusty— into the baker's garden.

The door of the baker's shop was open, the windows lighted. The full moon was shining. Jannot saw only the moon. And he jumped as high and as far as he could, he felt so happy. Over poppies, marigold and sweet william he jumped, and over china asters, pansies and peonies.

Suddenly in the middle of a sandy path, made all white by the moonlight, he stopped. What was that? Just facing him there was another—but bigger black rabbit.

Jannot stood on his hind legs. The big rabbit stood on his hind legs.

Jannot hopped; the big one hopped. And one hop to the left, and one hop to the right . . . and turn around . . . Jannot had found a partner for dancing in the moonlight—his own shadow.

He jumped into a bed of turnips and looked back.

Was the other one coming along?

Yes he was. But how long and big he had grown all of a sudden! And who was there, following him? The baker! His strong bare arms were white with flour, his face was red from the oven heat and from anger. He was looking around fiercely.

Bakers bake bread at night and a rabbit should not dance in their gardens by moonlight, at least not when he has a bell tied around his neck.

But Jannot crouched between two rows of turnips, ears down, eyes closed, white feet hidden under him.

The baker, angry and disappointed, had to go back to his bread baking.

He was still angry the next day when he woke up around noon. He went into the shop to talk to his wife. She was selling bread.

"I wonder," he said, "who was shaking a bell in my garden, last night!"

"And I wonder," replied his wife, "who broke my peonies and trampled my sweet william all over!"

Little Paul, who had come to buy fresh bread for lunch, overheard this talk.

A nice little boy does not listen to grown-ups' talk. He says politely, "Good-by ladies and gentlemen," when he leaves a store, and he brings the bread home right away. Well, Paul was a nice little boy, but that day, he listened to the baker's words as if he had wanted to eat them. He ran wildly out of the store. And with his long, fresh and easy to break bread under his arm, he rushed to Jannot's house.

And this was only the beginning! Ann and Paul, as soon as they realized what had happened, discussed what they could do to bring Jannot back. One thing they were sure of—they would tell no one about their discovery. They must find Jannot all by themselves.

Ann and Paul went to the baker's wife. They asked for a bunch of sweet william, which Ann explained she wanted to bring to her grandmother. As she spoke, her face got very red. But the good woman only complained that her flowers had been trampled by some "hooligan" the night before. She would be glad to give Ann what was left, she said. And while she was cutting the flowers, Ann and Paul investigated her garden thoroughly.

But Jannot had moved on to the blacksmith's garden at dawn. And there he was perfectly contented.

The blacksmith, a huge man, ate a lot of cabbage to make himself strong. In his garden there was one tender green cabbage head after one tender green cabbage head. Enough to make any rabbit want to stay. And if it had not been for music, Jannot would have stayed forever.

But one evening, a terrific noise broke out. A noise that made him push one ear and one eye through two pickets of the fence.

Pompom, Pompom, Pompom . . . trahideriderra . . .

The firemen marched down Main Street. They wore great shiny copper helmets and blue and red uniforms, and they blew mightily into their trumpets, their horns, their clarinets, and they beat their drums.

17

All the way down Main Street, they marched and passed the blacksmith's.

Behind them came boys and the girls carrying small birch trees in which hung yellow and red round lanterns.

Ann and Paul were among them. They each carried a lovely small tree with a yellow lantern. They were very proud, and so busy that they did not think of Jannot for one minute.

Then followed everyone in the village who had two legs and could walk.

The first firecracker exploded. Dogs howled in dark corners, cats jumped into trees and upon stone walls, Jannot Rabbit almost fainted. But he was even more afraid of the howling dogs than of the firecrackers, so after a few had been fired, Jannot squeezed through the pickets of the fence and got out of the garden. He hopped along behind the parade, his long ears pointed towards the sky in wonder. He gladly took part in the great national celebration of Bastille day.

Pompom, Pompom, Pompom . . .

Kling kling, kling kling, kling kling. . . .

When the parade stopped at the end of Main Street and more fireworks were sent off, the crowd cheered. Jannot thought all the stars of heaven were falling on him, and he forced his way under a nearby gate. He hid in some prickly shrubs and closed his eyes. And he kept them closed long after the stars had stopped falling and all the noises had died away, because he had fallen asleep. He was very tired.

Then the sky turned gray and pink. The birds began to sing. Jannot opened his eyes. Large golden roses and great white lilies were shedding on him scented drops of dew. He was in the priest's garden.

This was the most beautiful, the most bountiful, the most peaceful garden in the village.

The priest was old. He walked about in the shade of pear and apple trees, reading. And no bell and no rabbit could disturb him. Perhaps he did not see or hear very well.

20

But his housekeeper had eyes and ears for two and a good tongue for talking about all she saw and heard. One evening, at dusk, she met Ann and her mother on their way to the grocery store. The two ladies had a good chat. Ann, holding her mother's hand, waited politely. Suddenly she felt her ears burning.

"Yes," whispered the priest's housekeeper, "a tinkle bell. For the past three nights. I am quite sure. To me it sounds just as if a lost soul were wandering around the house."

Ann wanted to run like a wild horse, but a little girl who goes shopping with her mother cannot possibly do such a thing. Her thoughts, however, can run as wildly as they want. Ann saw herself running into the priest's garden. No, she saw herself jumping—no, flying—over the walls. And Jannot hopped right into her arms, and she carried him home, and. . . . And she knew all that was impossible. She looked helplessly at the high stone walls that surrounded the priest's garden.

At last Ann was able to meet Paul. They had a long, desperate talk. There was no way to get into the garden without telling their secret, or telling a lie. One could lie to the baker's wife, but one could not lie to the priest. Their secret Ann and Paul wanted to keep. And that was it—no way out.

The two children did discover a door that connected, no one knows why, the priest's garden with the grocer's garden. The grocer was not only a grocer, but a hunter, and a clever one.

Well, there was only one thing to do: pray that Jannot would not gnaw at the bottom of the door, which was old and soft, or dig a hole under it.

And that is just what Jannot did. Adventurous Jannot, he managed to get into the grocer's garden. Through every window he could see stuffed owls and stuffed foxes. A deer's foot was dangling from the doorbell. He smelled at the skins turned inside out that were hanging to dry by the back door. He could not possibly like such things. No, what he liked so much in this garden, what made him stay longer than he should, were the oyster plants. Hunters always grow oyster plants because they taste so good in rabbit stew.

One day, early in the morning, the grocer-hunter shouldered his shotgun and waited by his back door, for he knew there was a rabbit in his garden. He did not have long to wait. He heard a noise on his right, near the oyster plant bed; then almost at the same time a tinkling bell on his left. Who has ever heard of a rabbit tinkling a bell? The hunter thought he was dreaming. But he shot anyway. "Bang!" toward the right. "Kling kling," "Bang, bang, bang!"

"Kling, kling . . . kling, kling. . . ."

There never was a more puzzled hunter. So puzzled that he could not move for half a minute and so did not see a black thing, wildly shaking a bell, shoot behind him into his house. Jannot galloped down the hall and out through the front door as if he had always known the way.

He nearly flew along Main Street and came to a stop finally on the granite steps before the church portal. And there, the first rays of the good sun soothed his agitated mind and quieted the beating of his heart.

Then, quietly, before the church sexton tolled the Angelus bell, Jannot hopped down the steps into the cemetery that lay around the church. It was a lovely place, respected by people and dogs alike, where Ann and Paul never thought of looking.

They looked everywhere else, however. All day long they searched hedges and ditches for Jannot's body, because they were sure the shooting had been at Jannot.

They found nothing, not even a little bit of black fur! And they gave up their last hope. They were sad and tired when they went toward home that evening. Just as they passed the church, a thunderstorm broke. They ran toward the church porch for shelter.

And Jannot, who was in the cemetery, did the same. He was the first to reach the porch. He did not get even one drop of rain.

There was an empty niche under the statue of John the Baptist that had been made, apparently, for the statue of a rabbit, because Jannot fitted it exactly. By the time Ann and Paul got under cover their rabbit was well hidden and the rain was pouring.

"I'm sure I heard the bell'," said Ann. But Paul had heard nothing.

Then the sky turned black, the lightning flashed, the thunder rolled. Every other noise was stilled.

Besides Ann, Paul and Jannot, there were six statues of saints in the porch.

24

The saints, in their long robes of stone, looked fine on Sundays when people were around. But now, in the glare of lightning, they grew as tall as giants, and they smiled strangely.

When the rain stopped Ann and Paul went home,
holding each other's hands.

They did not look back.

The next morning, Jannot, tired of crouching in a
statue niche, hopped across the cemetery and over
the low stone wall.

He stopped in a narrow street and just at that moment the postman on his bicycle came around the corner. Jannot went galloping down the street. Kling-kling, klingety kling, through an open gate, into the mayor's garden.

But the postman was just as surprised as the rabbit. Where did that tinkling bell come from? There was no other bicycle around.

The postman was a man who wanted to understand things. He entered the little cafe on the corner and ordered a cup of strong black coffee and a glass, the size of a thimble, full of rum.

"I wonder," he said to the man behind the counter, "who was shaking a bell around here when I rode down the street. I could not see anyone."

"A bell? Maybe you need to wake up, postman," said the man behind the counter, and he offered him another tiny glass of rum, which the postman refused. It was getting late, he said, and he had a heavy bag of letters to distribute.

But all morning, as he rode around, he wondered and wondered about the bell.

In the meantime, Jannot was discovering the Mayor's garden. This was a good garden. It was large and rather neglected because the Mayor had no time for gardening. There was an empty burrow hidden in the tall grass, and there were some holes in the fence. Very convenient indeed. Jannot established himself for good. He went out twice a week, for a change, but he always came back.

He explored the butcher's garden, but it had poor vegetables, poor flowers, and a nasty smell.

He explored the constable's garden, a restless place.
The constable's wife, who was afraid of thieves, wandered about house and garden every night, carrying
a lamp in one hand and the fire tongs in the other.

He began slowly to take on the habits and the appearance of a settled bachelor. He gained weight, which he would not have done if he had known what was going on in the village. But how could a rabbit guess what was going on in people's minds?

The fact is that too many people had been puzzled about his bell.

One evening, the strong baker, the swift postman and the clever grocer, playing cards with the Mayor in the little cafe around the corner, were talking about the tinkling bell.

The Mayor laughed heartily.

"I know," he said. "I can tell you who shakes the bell: a wandering soul. Ah, ah, ah."

And he was not impressed that the butcher's wife, and the constable's wife, and even the teacher's wife had also heard the bell.

"Clever men like you," he said to his companions, "should not repeat such nonsense."

He went home smiling.

It was quite late. There was a golden crescent moon just on the top of the church tower, and millions of stars in the sky.

The Mayor paused before his door and looked quietly at the beautiful September night.

Kling, kling, kling, kling. . . .

Kling, kling. . . . The Mayor hurried into his house.

And the next morning everyone could see it, something had been set into motion.

At ten o'clock the Constable was standing in the middle of the town square beating his drum with a great show of energy. People appeared at every window.

Then the Constable, with his loud cheerful voice, read the Mayor's announcement: "The peace-loving people of this community have been disturbed in their sleep lately, by a hooligan who goes around mostly in gardens, shaking a bell.

"We, Mayor of this peace-loving community, advise strongly the trouble maker to stop at once.

"If he does not stop, and if he is caught—and we will do everything in our power to catch him—he will pay a fine that certainly will make him wiser."

After that, everyone was on the watch—men, women, children and dogs. Brooms and sticks were behind every door. And since this happened just before the opening of the hunting season, guns too, oiled and clean and shiny, were ready. Because people thought the trouble maker probably was a bad boy, they had put only coarse salt in the guns. But that was bad enough. Ann and Paul were in despair. Their Jannot was alive. But what was the good of being alive if the whole village was after him?

Ann and Paul walked sadly along fences and hedges and whispered, hoping Jannot would hear them, "Please Jannot stay quiet. Jannot dear, don't shake your head."

At the end of September, the Mayor gave his usual big hunting party. More than twenty hunters came to his house for a terrific twelve course dinner. They arrived four or five at a time in late afternoon. They had loud voices and carried their shot guns. From their big leather bags partridges and wild rabbits were dangling upside down. Their dogs followed close at their heels.

Jannot, at the farthest end of the garden, wiggled his nose with great anxiety. And a good reason he had to wiggle his nose. Three yelping dogs rushed into the garden. But Jannot also rushed, out through the back door.

Before him was the meadow: a wide, green, yellow, red racing carpet stretching from the woods to the river.

Blind with fear, Jannot started downhill and bumped into a big brown thing lying in the grass. The big brown thing got up and mooed. Jannot turned around and ran back up the hill.

Two of the dogs gave up chasing him. But the third one was dangerously close. Jannot then used a rabbit trick. He made a sudden right turn, ran a way, then made a sudden left turn, ran a way, and kept this up. They zigzagged through a field of crimson clover, and the dog lost ground at each unexpected turn.

Finally Jannot reached the forest and disappeared.

There was a sign at the edge of the forest which read, "No hunting allowed."

The dog stopped under the sign and peered into the darkness of the woods, whimpering and sad. Then he went back to the house with his two companions. They sat behind their masters' chairs, eating the bones that were thrown to them.

Jannot was in the forest. He wandered among great oaks and beech trees. He nibbled at new plants and drank from cool springs. He slept under lacy ferns and purple heather, jumped and bounced on beds of soft moss and got dizzy from fresh air and happiness.

Red squirrels came down from tree tops, looked at him, danced away and sometimes scolded him.

Birds followed him with shrill calls.

Jannot did not worry about the opinions of squirrels or small birds. But one dark night the Great Owl discovered him. He silently flew down from a tree top fanning the air with his dust-gray wings, and lighting the night with his gold-green eyes.

Jannot could not make out what that was and he shook his head vigorously to keep his ideas clear. His bell tinkled smartly.

The owl hovered over him for a moment, then flew away.

A few days later, shortly after dawn, he was sniffing at the east wind, when suddenly he smelled a strong, strange musky odor, that meant "Danger." Jannot crouched against a dark tree trunk. His eyes were wide open, and they grew wider when they caught sight of the Red Fox quietly coming toward him.

Jannot began to tremble. And so did his bell. The fox stopped and pricked his ears. And then his narrow, mean eyes spotted the rabbit. He stared at him and licked his chops. But the more he stared, the more frightened Jannot got, and the more he shook . . . and the more his bell tinkled.

The fox was all mixed up.

The hair on his neck and along his spine stood on end. Slowly he turned around and went back the way he had come.

At the first turn in the path he broke into a trot and was gone. . . .

One night, by moonlight, a wonderful thing happened. In a clearing Jannot discovered twenty or more wild rabbits frolicking in a bed of thyme and marjoram. They had brown coats and their tails and bellies were snow white.

Jannot crawled silently into a corner and stayed there, motionless. But he was tall, dark, and handsome. Two lovely ladies, their breath scented by the thyme they had been chewing, their pink noses fresh and cool from the dew, saw him and came very close indeed. Jannot, overcome with pride and joy, jumped mightily into the middle of the meeting. "Here I am, ladies!"

Kling, kling, kling, kling . . . tinkled the silver bell. No sooner had they heard the sound than away ran all the wild rabbits and their lovely ladies.

Jannot was left alone in the middle of the clearing.

And that ended Jannot's life in the forest. The next
day he left. He went through fields and meadows
until he came to a great building with walls and
towers covered with ivy. All around it was a moat filled
with water in which grew water lilies and weeds.
Across the moat was a drawbridge. Here was a castle
built hundreds of years before for a queen, but a queen
did not live in it any more. In the castle lived only
three ladies with their three maids, a gardener and
a cook—all of them very old.

Just as Jannot arrived at the castle, the old ladies,
with green veils over their faces, climbed into their
carriage. The gardener had put on a top hat and black
coat and he drove them klip-klop, klip-klop over the
bridge to the village. No one saw Jannot.

40

After the carriage and the horse had disappeared, Jannot started exploring. He found a lovely garden and trees and lawns. He decided to settle there.

It was a very peaceful home. No one ever came from the village, and except for the daily drive, no one ever left the castle. To be sure, the maids said they often heard the tinkling of a silver bell, and the old ladies said they had not rung.

"Our dear ladies are getting old," said the maids.

"Our dear maids are getting old," said the old ladies.

In the village things were quiet, too. The housewives had put away their brooms and sticks. The children were in school, and all the men were proud of the way they had frightened away the hooligan who had disturbed the village.

Ann and Paul had not forgotten Jannot, but they were busy with school. It was only on Sundays, when they went for a walk with their parents, that they had a chance to look for him. One cold November day, as they were walking in the woods, they talked about him.

"If he hid in the woods," said Paul, "the fox got him."

"Or the big owl," said Ann.

"We'll never see Jannot again," they said together.

In the castle garden, Jannot was cold. Food was scarce and he was tired of eating nothing but flowers. He had eaten all the patch of four-leaf clovers that the old ladies especially loved. At last Jannot made up his mind. He did not want to starve, even in a castle garden. So off he went, over the drawbridge, through the woods until he came to a hill above the village.

It was a gray, frosty, silent morning. One of those mornings when the dogs felt cold and wanted to stay indoors. Jannot went down the hill, faster perhaps, than he had planned, for a flock of crows, cawing as they came, flew toward him.

Down the hill he went till he was stopped by a garden fence. He searched for a hole, and when he found one, he squeezed through, leaving a bit of his winter fur coat on it.

44

He looked around at the garden. How familiar it seemed! This was where he had lived before he started on his adventures. This was home!

Jannot was happily munching on delicious Brussel sprouts when the garden gate opened. It was Ann. She stopped short when she saw him and turned and ran to Paul's house.

"Jannot," she cried, "Jannot's ghost is in the garden!"
Together the children ran back to Ann's house.
There was Jannot, munching away. It was no ghost
but a real, big, black rabbit.

Ann and Paul tiptoed to Jannot's old hutch. They made a bed of fresh yellow straw; they filled the bowls with water and carrots, the trough with fine scented hay; they left the door open and pretended to go away. And Jannot, as if he were waiting for that moment, quietly entered his house and started on a second breakfast.

"My, Jannot," said Ann, "how big you have grown and how wise!"

"Rabbits are wiser than you think," said Paul, "but I wonder how he found food and never ate any 'bad grass.'"

"Rabbits are wiser than you think," Ann said, and both the children laughed.

They took off the collar from the rabbit's neck. It had really become too small for such a big rabbit.

Jannot shook his head many times, relieved indeed and looking very much like a rabbit who thinks, "My, children, how wise you have grown in one summer!"